For our Little Mate

This edition copyright © 2001
Baby's First Book Club®
Bristol, PA 19007

Originally published in Great Britain 1997 by
Little Tiger Press, London
An imprint of Magi Publications

Text and illustrations © 1997 Catherine Walters

All rights reserved • Printed in Belgium
ISBN 1-58048-142-6

When will it be Spring?

"Come inside, Alfie," said Mother Bear. "It's time to sleep, and when you wake up it will be spring."

"When will it be spring?" asked Alfie. "And how will I know when it's here?"

Mother Bear replied, "When the butterflies float by looking for new flowers, then it will be spring."

So Alfie snuggled down to sleep...

. . . but when he woke up, Alfie could not tell if spring had come or not. He tiptoed across the floor of the cave, rubbed his bleary eyes, and saw. . .

BUTTERFLIES!

"It's spring! It's spring!" cried Alfie.
"Wake up, Mother! I see a big gray
butterfly and lots of little white ones!"

But when Mother Bear came out, she could only see the soft fall of new snow.

"Winter has hardly begun," she said. "Go back to sleep, Alfie."

"But when *will* it be spring?" Alfie wanted to know.

And Mother Bear mumbled sleepily, "When the swallows arrive, and there are birds in every tree. *Then* it will be spring."

Then Alfie curled up
again to sleep...

...and when he woke
he was sure it must
be time for spring.

He crept across the floor,
peered outside, and saw...

BIRDS IN THE TREES!

"Mother, wake up!" squealed Alfie.
"Spring is here! The swallows have come.
And they are singing in the trees!"

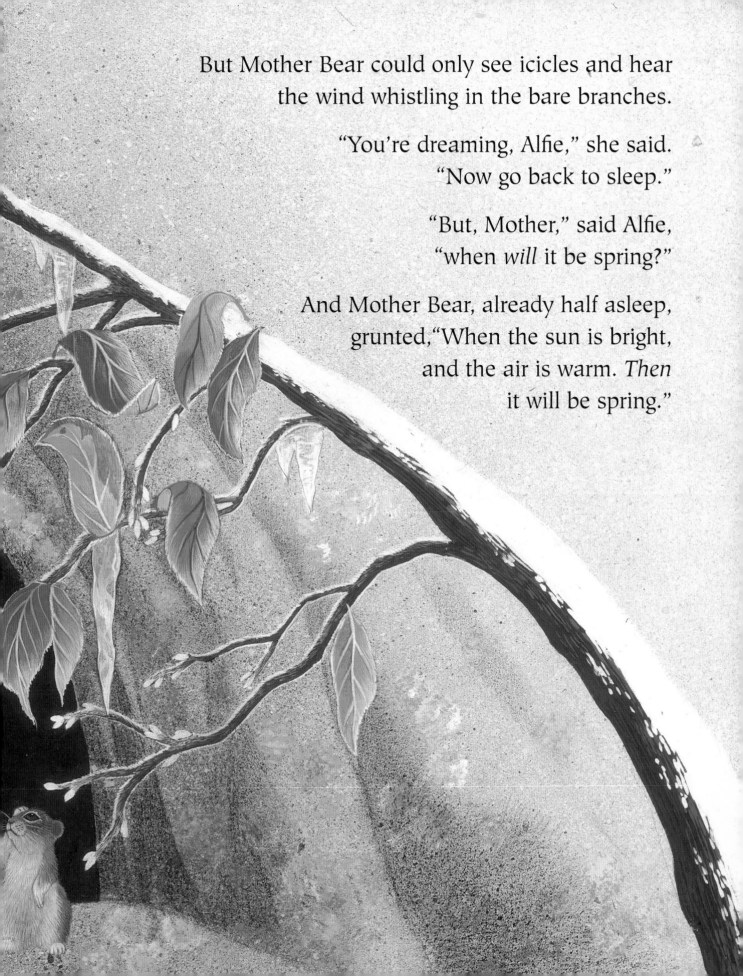

But Mother Bear could only see icicles and hear
the wind whistling in the bare branches.

"You're dreaming, Alfie," she said.
"Now go back to sleep."

"But, Mother," said Alfie,
"when *will* it be spring?"

And Mother Bear, already half asleep,
grunted, "When the sun is bright,
and the air is warm. *Then*
it will be spring."

So Alfie burrowed down in his bed again...

. . . and when he woke, he was quite sure spring was here.
He padded across the floor, looked out, and saw. . .

A BRIGHT SUN!

"Mother, you've overslept!" cried Alfie. "Wake up! Spring is here. The sun is shining and it's getting warm!"

But Mother Bear could only see
the hunters' fires and quickly
hustled her cub away.

"Now go to sleep!" she said.
"I will tell you when spring is here."

So Alfie slept and dreamed of butterflies, birds, and sunshine until something icy touched his nose! A tiny stream of water was trickling through the cave.

Alfie shook his mother awake and she growled, "For the last time, Alfie, it is *not* spring."

But Alfie patted her
hopefully until she got up,
stomped through
the doorway,

and saw...

SPRING!

Mother Bear rubbed her eyes and blinked in the warm, bright light.

"Spring is here after all," she said with a smile. "But *where* is Alfie?"